written by Na...

Papa & Nana
Almost Always
Say Yes

TATE PUBLISHING
& Enterprises

Published by Tate Publishing & Enterprises, LLC
127 E. Trade Center Terrace | Mustang, Oklahoma 73064 USA
1.888.361.9473 | www.tatepublishing.com

Tate Publishing is committed to excellence in the publishing industry. The company reflects the philosophy established by the founders, based on Psalm 68:11,
"The Lord gave the word and great was the company of those who published it."

Book design copyright © 2010 by Tate Publishing, LLC. All rights reserved.
Cover and interior design by Scott Parrish
Illustrations by Jesse Warne

Published in the United States of America

ISBN: 978-1-61663-822-1
1. Juvenile Fiction / Family / Multigenerational
2. Juvenile Fiction / Religious / Christian / Family
10.11.23

Dedication

This book is dedicated to my grandchildren,
those born and those yet to be born.

I love to go to Papa and Nana's house. Mommy says the rules at their house are different than ours. When Papa sees me, he says, "Hi, you little rug rat." When Nana sees me, she says "Hello, Angel."

Papa lets me eat cookie dough ice cream in the morning. He smiles and whispers, "Don't tell Nana," but I think Nana already knows.

I like to help Nana cook. I stand on a chair and put in a bowl what she cuts up with a knife. She lets me toss salad and dump stuff like flour and sugar in the cookie dough. I tell her if the dough is good or not.

I like to play in Papa's truck. He sits in the truck with me, and I pretend to drive him around. Sometimes, I climb in and out of the window that goes to the back of the truck.

Nana makes up stories and lets me name the characters. She will read the same book over and over. When we go to the park, we stay until I am tired.

When we go out in Papa's boat, I have to wear a life jacket, but he lets me jump off the side of the boat into the lake. He says it's all right for me to swing really high and hold onto the monkey bars with just one hand. He doesn't care if I get dirty or go outside without my shoes.

When we go out in Nana's garden, she lets me pick lots of flowers. She says that is what they are for. When we take the flowers into the house, I get to pick a vase to put them in.

I like to sleep with Papa and Nana. Sometimes, Papa's snoring wakes me up, and I don't like that. I tickle Nana when I wake up in the morning. She says people shouldn't get up before the sun, but she gets up anyway. I tickle Papa, but he doesn't wake up.

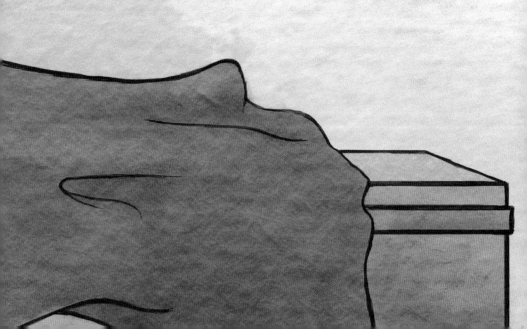

Nana smells like flowers, and Papa smells like Life Savers. I like to snuggle with them when we watch a movie. I always get to pick the movie and hold the bowl of popcorn.

Papa and Nana buy a swimming pool every summer so I can play in the water when I come to visit. They put the pool in the driveway. One day, after I went home, Nana forgot the pool was still in the driveway, and she backed over it with her car. I told her she was silly for doing that, and she agreed.

Most gifts come wrapped up in pretty paper with a bow, but some do not. Papa and Nana say that I am a gift to them from God. I think they are God's gift to me.

The End

listen|imagine|view|experience

AUDIO BOOK DOWNLOAD INCLUDED WITH THIS BOOK!

In your hands you hold a complete digital entertainment package. In addition to the paper version, you receive a free download of the audio version of this book. Simply use the code listed below when visiting our website. Once downloaded to your computer, you can listen to the book through your computer's speakers, burn it to an audio CD or save the file to your portable music device (such as Apple's popular iPod) and listen on the go!

How to get your free audio book digital download:

1. Visit www.tatepublishing.com and click on the e|LIVE logo on the home page.
2. Enter the following coupon code:
   c32e-3573-805b-4906-76d0-756c-e2d7-2cf2
3. Download the audio book from your e|LIVE digital locker and begin enjoying your new digital entertainment package today!